# Best Enemies FOREVER

That night at dinner Priscilla told her family what had happened. "Felicity said there were two kinds of people: stars like her and ordinary little people like me."

Priscilla's dog, Pow-wow, growled under the table.

"Haven't you learned by now?" said Priscilla's big sister, Eve. "*Never listen to Felicity.*"

# KATHLEEN LEVERICH

# Best Enemies FOREVER

**Illustrated by Walter Lorraine**

Beech Tree
New York

The Library of Congress has cataloged the Greenwillow Books edition of
*Best Enemies Forever* as follows:
Leverich, Kathleen.
Best enemies forever / by Kathleen Leverich; pictures by Walter Lorraine.
p. cm.
Summary: When Priscilla starts a school club to provide volunteer service
to the community, her project comes under fire from her longtime enemy
Felicity, who wants to be the only star in the fourth grade.
ISBN 0-688-13963-9
[1. Schools—Fiction.   2. Clubs—Fiction.   3. Volunteerism—Fiction.]
I. Lorraine, Walter H., ill.   II. Title.   PZ7.L5744Beg 1995
[Fic]—dc20   94-26790   CIP   AC

First Beech Tree Edition, 1998
ISBN 0-688-15854-4
10 9 8 7 6 5 4 3 2 1

For

ELVA LORRAINE

1 9 0 2 – 1 9 9 3

# Contents

# 1 The Club

That September afternoon Priscilla Robin sat at
her desk and watched the clock. Only five minutes
more in the school day. Only five minutes more in
the school week. Only five more minutes until the
best weekend of the autumn would begin.

"Let's talk about weekend plans," said Mr. Piper.
"Who's doing something special?"

Priscilla shot up her hand.

Priscilla's big sister, Eve, belonged to a high
school club, the Hi-5s. The Hi-5s did things to help

the community. They cleaned up the vacant lot on
Summit Road so it could be used for a park. They
ran errands for people who were sick and couldn't
go out. Their slogan was, One for all and all for
one! This weekend they were holding a car wash.
It would raise money for the town library. Even
though the Hi–5s were big kids, they'd invited Priscilla to help.

Priscilla held her arm high. She looked straight at
Mr. Piper. The school year had just started, but
already Priscilla liked Mr. Piper better than any
teacher she'd ever had. She wanted Mr. Piper to like
her. The Hi–5 car wash might be a start.

"Ariel," said Mr. Piper. "Let's hear from you."

Ariel Gump stood. "My brother and I are taking
five cartons of bottles to the recycling center. We
get to smash whatever we bring."

"That's good for the environment," said Mr.
Piper. "Anyone else?"

Priscilla raised her hand as high as she could. She
hoped that when the kids in her class heard about
Hi–5s, they'd want to start a club just like it.

"Jocko," said Mr. Piper. "What are your plans?"

Jocko stood. "First, my parents and I are going to paint my bedroom—"

"The bell hasn't rung yet, Jocko," said Mr. Piper. "Take off your baseball cap before you say another word."

Priscilla watched Jocko pull off his black and silver cap and stuff it into his back pocket. Hi-5 members wore caps, too. Bright red ones. They were allowed to wear them even in school. The caps made it easy for people to spot the Hi-5s and ask for help.

"We're painting my room silver with black trim. Those are the colors of my uncle's motorcycle," said Jocko. "Tomorrow night, while the paint dries, I get to sleep on a cot in the den. Otherwise I might breathe in fumes and throw up."

Mr. Piper said, "Sleeping in a different room is always exciting. Anyone else?"

Priscilla raised her hand. She'd be sleeping in a different room, too. Eve was giving a slumber party after the car wash. All the Hi-5 girls were coming. Priscilla was going to stay up late with them. She was going to sleep in a sleeping bag in the living room.

She waved her arm to get the teacher's attention. Mr. Piper nodded at her. "Yes, Priscil—"

"Mr. Piper!" said the person sitting behind Priscilla. "I have something important to tell you. Can I go next? *Pleeease?*"

Mr. Piper looked startled.

"I wouldn't interrupt, but I have to leave early"—the person sighed—"for a dentist appointment."

Mr. Piper smiled. "That's an excuse we all understand. You'll let Felicity go first, won't you, Priscilla?"

Priscilla's heart sank. *Felicity*. Felicity Doll.

Felicity had been in Priscilla's class since first grade. Since first grade she'd made Priscilla's life miserable. She made fun of Priscilla's clothes. She stole her ideas. She messed up her birthdays—

"*Pleeease*, Priscilla?" said Felicity.

Priscilla turned to look at her. Felicity's curly hair made a golden halo around her head. Ruffles covered her red plaid dress. Ruffles covered every piece of clothing Felicity owned. When parents and teachers were around, Felicity acted polite. Sincere. Perfect. When she and Priscilla were alone, Felicity acted like a snake.

"Priscilla?" said Mr. Piper. "What do you think?"

Priscilla didn't know what to say. She didn't want to be mean, but there were only a few minutes left.

She wanted time to tell about her weekend.

"Priscilla?"

"Never mind," said Felicity. "*I*'d let Priscilla go first. But some people are a *teeny* bit selfish."

"I'm not selfish!" Priscilla's cheeks flamed. She looked from Felicity to Mr. Piper. "Felicity can go first."

"Oboy!" Felicity leaped to her feet. She fluffed her ruffles. "On Saturday my dance class is having a recital. 'Salute to Autumn.' I'm going to dance the final solo. 'The Beauteous Autumn Tree.' It's part tap, part ballet, and part jazz. My teacher calls it the showstopper."

"Isn't that exciting?" said Mr. Piper. "Are any other class members in this recital?"

Pam raised her hand. So did Jason and Julianne.

"Others are *in* the recital," said Felicity. "Because it takes lots of ordinary little people to put on a show. But I guess you'd have to say"—she lowered her head as if she were embarrassed—"I'm the star."

"Congratulations!" said Mr. Piper.

Priscilla couldn't stand it. Didn't Mr. Piper see

that Felicity was bragging? Didn't he see that she was showing off? How could he be fooled . . .

Maybe he's not being fooled, thought Priscilla. Maybe I'm being jealous. . . .

"We'll look forward to hearing on Monday how the recital went," said Mr. Piper. "Meanwhile, Priscilla wants to share her weekend plans."

Priscilla scrambled to her feet. "This weekend—"

The bell rang.

Felicity called out, "Mr. Piper, I'd *love* to listen to Priscilla, but I have that dentist appointment. May I be excused?"

"Of course," said Mr. Piper. "Anyone who must leave may. The rest of us will keep our seats until Priscilla finishes."

Kids all around Priscilla pushed back their chairs.

"This weekend I'm helping with a car wash," said Priscilla.

Kids all around her grabbed their books.

"My sister and her friends are in a school club called Hi-5s."

Kids grabbed their jackets and headed for the door.

"I'm going to scrub tires . . ." Priscilla's voice trailed off.

No one was there to hear her.

Everyone but the teacher had left.

"I'm sorry everyone ran off," said Mr. Piper.

Priscilla shrugged. "It's not important. I don't care."

But she did care. She cared a lot.

Mr. Piper patted her shoulder. "It sounds as though you have a worthwhile weekend planned. On Monday we'll be eager to hear all about it."

Priscilla felt warm where the teacher's hand rested on her shoulder. She looked up at him.

Mr. Piper smiled at her.

Priscilla felt warm all over. *A worthwhile weekend . . . We'll be eager to hear . . .*

Priscilla couldn't wait for Monday. She gathered her books and jacket and left.


Priscilla hopped down the school steps. She skipped along the sidewalk.

"Hey, Robin Redbreast!" someone called from the playground.

Priscilla turned to look.

Felicity leaned against the giant willow tree.

"I thought you were going to the dentist," said Priscilla.

Felicity bared two rows of sparkling white teeth. "This star doesn't need to see a dentist. This star has perfect teeth."

"But you said you couldn't listen to me. You had to leave," said Priscilla.

Felicity gave her ruffles a fluff. "This star doesn't have time to listen to an ordinary little person. Not while she brags about working in a car wash."

"I wasn't bragging," said Priscilla.

"I guess not," said Felicity. "I wouldn't brag if I had to spend my weekend washing dirty cars."

"But I want to do it!" said Priscilla. "It's fun to do things with Eve and her club. They wear red caps. They help other people. They have a slogan. One for all and all for one!"

"Want to hear my slogan?" said Felicity. "All for me and me for myself!"

Priscilla blinked. "That sounds selfish."

Felicity smiled a snaky smile. "It is selfish. A star has to be selfish. To stand apart from ordinary little people like you."

Priscilla frowned. She tried again. "I'm going to start a club at our school. It's going to be just like Hi-5s. I bet lots of kids will join. Maybe even you."

"Stars don't join clubs," said Felicity. "Stars *have* clubs. Fan clubs. If you want a club, start one of those for me."

That night at dinner Priscilla told her family what had happened. "Felicity said there were two kinds of people: stars like her and ordinary little people like me."

Priscilla's dog, Pow-wow, growled under the table.

"Haven't you learned by now?" said Priscilla's big sister, Eve. *"Never listen to Felicity."*

"I try not to listen," said Priscilla. "But Felicity has a way of talking. I can't help but hear."

"Next time cover your ears," said her father.

"Leave next time," said her mother. "Just walk away."

Priscilla pushed lima beans around her plate. Everyone thought it should be easy to ignore Felicity. As long as she was sitting at her own dinner table in her own house with her own family, Priscilla thought so, too. But in real life, at school—

Priscilla looked at her mother. "Am I ordinary?"

Her mother patted her hand. "You're just fine."

"We wouldn't want you to be like Felicity," said her father. "Star or not."

Eve giggled. "There's only one way to be like Felicity. That's to flick your tongue and slither along the ground."

"Eve!" said her mother.

"Let's not be unkind," said her father.

"It's the truth," said Eve. "Felicity is a real snake."

The following afternoon Priscilla squatted beside a blue station wagon. She gave its rear wheel one final scrub with her soapy sponge.

Pow-wow sniffed the soap suds. He sniffed the tire.

"Ready?" cried Eve.

"Ready!" called Priscilla.

Eve pointed her hose at the back of the car.

Water sprayed off the fender.

It hit Pow-wow in the tail.

It hit Priscilla in the face.

"Sorry!" said Eve. "I didn't mean to spray so hard."

Pow-wow shook himself.

Priscilla wiped her face on her sleeve and grinned. She didn't mind getting sprayed. She was wearing her oldest jeans, her oldest sweatshirt, and sneakers. She already was damp and dirty from scrubbing so many tires. Besides, being a mess today was sort of fun. It showed she'd worked hard. It showed she was one of the Hi-5s. At least for this weekend.

Being a mess wasn't all that showed it. Eve and the others had given Priscilla something for helping. She reached a hand up to touch it. A bright red Hi-5 cap. Priscilla felt so proud she couldn't stop grinning. She couldn't wait for Monday to try to start her own club.

"Hey, you! Tire scrubber!"

Priscilla saw a silver sedan pull into the car wash space beside her. A glamorous girl stepped out of it. Lipstick reddened the girl's lips. Her cheeks were rosy with blusher. Makeup made her eyes look big and green. Her false eyelashes were long and curly.

Pow-wow raised his ruff and barked.

The glamorous girl said, "What's wrong, ordinary little dog? Haven't you ever seen a star?"

That voice wasn't the least bit glamorous. That voice was loud and familiar.

Priscilla rubbed her eyes and looked again.

That girl really was Felicity.

Felicity wore black ballet slippers, tree-bark brown tights, a tree-bark brown leotard, and a ruffly tutu made of red, orange, and gold "leaves." Glitter sparkled in her hair. Sunlight shimmered on her ruffly tutu.

Felicity fluffed the leaves. "They're silk with spangles. Five parents worked ten hours to make them."

Priscilla stood in her damp, dirty clothes. Her wet hair clung stringily to her head. She felt grimy. She felt plain. She couldn't stop looking at Felicity.

"Do a good job on those tires." Felicity tossed her glittery hair as she walked away. "Curtain time is in half an hour. I want my car to shine as brightly as I do."

Priscilla scrubbed the grimy tires until they shone. She polished the dull hubcaps until they gleamed. She didn't do it because of Felicity. She washed every car that way. The shinier the tires got and the more the hubcaps gleamed, the more something inside Priscilla gleamed and shone, too.

Eve and the others washed the car's hood, fenders, windows, and trunk. They hosed it off. They toweled it dry. All of them stood back to look.

The car sparkled.

"You Hi-5s did *almost* as good a job as the automatic car wash." Felicity's mother climbed into the front seat.

"You charge more than the automatic car wash. But I suppose it's for a good cause." Felicity's father climbed into the front seat, too.

Felicity climbed into the back. She opened her window and leaned out. "So long, faceless masses."

Priscilla watched Felicity's car glide down the street. She thought about Felicity in her silk, sparkles, and makeup. She wished that she could be as—

"Let's go, Hi-5s!" said Eve. "Next car."

Priscilla shook herself. She couldn't believe she'd wished—even for a second—to be *anything* like Felicity.

"C'mon, Pow-wow." Priscilla picked up her sponge and went back to work.

That night at the slumber party Eve and the others popped popcorn. They watched movies on the VCR. They fixed one another's hair in new ways.

Priscilla helped them do all those things. While she helped, she planned how she'd tell her class all about it on Monday. She planned how she'd say, Why don't we start a club, too . . . ?

"Priscilla's next," said Jennifer. "What should we do with her hair?"

"We could color it," said Michelle.

Michelle's hair was green with blue streaks. If Priscilla had hair like that, no one would join her club. She shook her head. "I like my hair the color it is."

"We could give Priscilla a haircut," said Lauri.

Lauri's hair was shorter than a boy's. If Priscilla's hair looked like that, no one would join her club. She covered her head. "I like my hair long."

The phone rang.

Melissa answered. "Hey, Priscilla, it's for you."

Priscilla took the phone. "Hello?"

"Here's a star flash for you, ordinary little person—"

Priscilla remembered what her family had said: "Don't listen to Felicity. Don't talk to her."

"My recital was a giant success! I'm going to wear my star tap shoes on Monday when I tell about it. I'm going to wear star glitter in my hair. What are you going to wear to tell about your car wash? Your grimy sweatshirt? Your wet, stringy hair?"

"I have to go." Priscilla hung up the phone. She hadn't listened for long, but it had been long enough. Felicity was right. No one would join a club started by an ordinary little person. The only special thing Priscilla had for Monday was her cap. And she wouldn't be allowed to wear that.

"We could give Priscilla a body perm," Eve was saying.

"What do you think, Priscilla?" said Stephanie.

Priscilla didn't know anything about body perms. She was busy worrying about her club. "How would that make my hair look?"

"The same," said Margaret. "But with more bounce."

Priscilla thought of Felicity walking into school Monday morning with her hair full of glitter. She thought of Felicity tapping down the hall in her tap shoes.

Priscilla imagined herself walking down the same hall with hair that bounced. Her classmates said, *Look at Priscilla! She looks different. She looks—not ordinary! If she started a club, I'd join. . . .*

"A body perm sounds okay," said Priscilla. "What do I have to do?"

"Nothing," said Jennifer.

"Put yourself in our hands," said Michelle.

"One for all and all for one!" said Amy. "The Hi-5s will take care of everything."

The Hi-5s did.

Eve mixed the lotion and combed it through Priscilla's hair.

Michelle divided Priscilla's hair into sections and wrapped each section around a curler.

After forty-five minutes Lauri took out the curlers and shampooed.

"When can I see it?" said Priscilla.

"You'll have plenty of time when it's dry," said Eve. "This permanent will last a whole month."

"If you're lucky," said Lauri, "two months!"

Jennifer dried Priscilla's hair with a dryer.

Lauri brushed.

Everyone else crowded around the bathroom to watch.

Priscilla sat in the middle of the group and felt great. She hoped the club she'd start would be just like this one. All the members would work hard on a project. When they finished, they'd celebrate.

"Is that the way it's *supposed* to look?"

The hair dryer made a lot of noise, but Priscilla heard the older girls' voices anyway.

"Brush it some more. That might help."

Jennifer turned off the dryer. "That's it, I guess."

Priscilla reached up to touch her hair. It felt bouncy. It felt more than bouncy. It felt like a new kind of hair. "Can I look in the mirror?"

Amy and Jennifer stepped out of the way.

Priscilla peered into the medicine cabinet mirror.

A strange girl peered back.

"You look different," said Lauri.

"Really different," said Michelle.

Priscilla was so shocked she could hardly speak.
The girl in the mirror had a halo of tight brown
curls.

"*Different* isn't the way I look," said Priscilla. "I
look like—I look—"

Eve sighed and said it for her. "You look like
Felicity."

"I'm afraid it's true," said Priscilla's father at
breakfast on Monday morning.

Her mother said, "If you were wearing ruffles, you could be Felicity's long-lost brown-haired twin."

"But Felicity looks normal with curls. Priscilla looks . . ." Eve let her voice trail off.

"How do I look?" said Priscilla.

"You don't look ordinary," said her mother. "That's for sure."

"I've never seen a permanent curl so much," said Eve. "Priscilla, you must have extra-sensitive hair."

"Let's not blame Priscilla," said her mother.

"I'll never get a club started now," said Priscilla. "Not when people see these curls."

"Just ignore the curls," said her father. "If you do, everyone else will."

Eve rolled her eyes.

Priscilla stood up from the table. "Felicity won't. Felicity will make sure everyone laughs at me." She pulled on her jacket. She pulled on her Hi-5s cap. She stuffed her curls underneath it.

"That's better," said her mother. "Your cap solves the problem."

"It won't solve it for long," said Priscilla. "We're not allowed to wear caps in school. When Mr. Piper makes me take off mine, everyone will see my hair. Everyone will laugh. Felicity will laugh loudest of all."

"Tell Mr. Piper the problem," said her father. "He's understanding. He'll let you wear the cap for the next little while."

Mr. Piper . . . thought Priscilla. He might . . .

"The next little while isn't long enough," said Eve. "That permanent will last a whole month."

Priscilla sighed. "If I'm lucky, *two* months."

"Oh, dear." Her parents shook their heads.

Priscilla kissed them good-bye and left for school.

Priscilla kept her head down as she hurried along the sidewalk. She kept her fingers crossed that no one would notice her. She got to school early, pulled open the heavy front door, and crept inside—

"Not so fast, ordinary little person!" Felicity stepped out of the shadows and into her path.

Glitter shone in Felicity's hair. Patent leather tap shoes gleamed on her feet. Felicity's pink skirt was covered with ruffles. Her pink socks were covered with ruffles. Her pink top didn't have any ruffles. Instead it had gold writing across the chest that said CLAP! I'M A SUPER— Underneath the writing shone a big gold glitter star.

"Why are you sneaking around?" Felicity tapped her foot. Her tap shoe made a loud, clicking noise that echoed in the hallway.

Priscilla straightened her cap. She tried to sound normal. "I wasn't sneaking."

Felicity looked her up and down. From Priscilla's ordinary shoes to her ordinary pants to her ordinary jacket. When she got to Priscilla's cap, she frowned. "Why do you have all your hair stuffed under that cap?" She smiled a snaky smile. "Is there something you're trying to hide?"

Priscilla felt the curls tighten under her cap.

"Well?" said Felicity.

Priscilla wiped her hands on her pants. "I'm not

hiding anything. I'm wearing the cap to help explain about the car wash. I stuffed my hair under to keep it out of my eyes."

Felicity gave Priscilla a hard look. She didn't seem convinced.

"And," said Priscilla, "I'm wearing the cap because of the club I'm going to start. Kids who join will wear caps, too." Priscilla wished Felicity would move out of her way. She wished that Felicity would stop looking at her cap. If Felicity guessed what was under it—

"Coming through!" Henry pushed past Priscilla and Felicity.

"No blocking the door!" Jocko pushed past them, too.

"Wait for me!" Priscilla pushed past Felicity and followed the boys down the hall.

"You're hiding something!" Felicity called after her. "When people get a look, they won't join your club. And they're going to get a look. I guarantee."

**A**s soon as class started, Mr. Piper said, "Many

of you have exciting weekends to tell us about. Who wants to go first?"

Priscilla raised her hand. She wanted to tell about the car wash. She wanted to tell about the Hi-5s. She wanted to ask if they could have a Hi-5 club—

Priscilla caught herself just in time.

If Mr. Piper called on her, he'd make her take off her cap.

Priscilla pulled down her hand. She scrunched it in her lap instead.

"Felicity," said Mr. Piper. "How did the dance recital go?"

Felicity stood. "I danced my personal best. Everyone clapped. I got three curtain calls and a bouquet of roses. I would have gotten even more curtain calls, but the teacher asked my relatives to stop clapping."

"You must have been a lovely autumn tree," said Mr. Piper. "We wish we could have seen you. Don't we, class?"

"*Ye-es,*" said everyone.

Priscilla said it, too, but she didn't mean it.

She hoped Mr. Piper didn't either.

"You *will* see," said Felicity. "My uncle made a video. *Felicity Dances*. Tomorrow I'll bring it to class and show it. In the meantime"—Felicity took a big brown envelope from her desk—"I have these photos of me. Posed. In costume. There's one for everybody. If people ask politely and don't push, I'll even autograph them."

"Isn't that fine?" said Mr. Piper. "Hand out the photos now. But let's save the autographing for after school."

Felicity walked up and down the rows of desks, handing out pictures. Glitter fell from her hair like stardust. Her taps tapped loud and clear.

Mary caught some of the glitter. "Cool!"

Raheem bent to look at Felicity's taps. "Neat!"

"It must be great to be a star," said Ariel. "I wish I were one."

When all the photos were gone, Felicity took her seat.

"We'll look forward to seeing your recital video," said Mr. Piper. "But tomorrow, no glitter and no

tap shoes. They're a distraction. Who else would like to speak?"

Priscilla scrunched deeper in her chair.

"*Pssst!*" whispered Felicity. "*You* wanted to tell about *your* weekend, Priscilla. Raise your ordinary little hand!"

Priscilla kept her hand in her lap. She was careful not to meet the teacher's eye.

"Raheem," said Mr. Piper. "Let's hear from you."

Priscilla let out her breath and relaxed.

Raheem's thumb was wrapped in a big bandage. He said, "On Sunday I helped my parents build bookshelves in our study. I tried to hammer a big nail, but I hammered my thumbnail instead. My dad says it's going to turn black. He says it might even fall off."

*"Ehwww!"* said everyone.

"Carpentry takes great skill and courage," said Mr. Piper. "Who'd like to go next?"

Priscilla scrunched lower. Only five minutes were left until math period. If Mr. Piper didn't call on her this time—

"Mr. Piper!" said Felicity.

"Felicity, you've already spoken," said Mr. Piper. "Let's hear from someone else."

"That's what I want to say!" said Felicity. "We're *dying* to hear about Priscilla's car wash. Let's hear from her."

Priscilla spun around to look at Felicity.

Felicity batted her eyelashes. She smiled a snaky smile.

"Thank you for reminding us," said Mr. Piper. "We didn't hear from Priscilla on Friday. Let's give her our full attention now. Priscilla?"

Priscilla felt the curls tighten under her cap. She stood and slowly began. "On Saturday—"

"Mr. Piper," said Felicity, "shouldn't Priscilla take off her cap?"

"That's right," said Jocko. "I couldn't wear *my* cap. Priscilla shouldn't get to wear hers."

"I think Priscilla is wearing her cap as a visual aid. She's wearing it to help explain her weekend." Mr. Piper smiled at Priscilla. "Isn't that right?"

Priscilla nodded. She pulled the cap lower on her head.

Mr. Piper said, "How did the Hi-5 car wash go?"

Priscilla put the curls from her mind and told. She told all about scrubbing tires. She told all about getting dirty and damp but still being in a good mood. She told all about "One for all and all for one!"

"Cool!" said Jocko.

"Neat!" said Ariel.

The more Priscilla told, the more excited she got.

"We raised one hundred and seventeen dollars for the library. The Hi-5 girls came to our house for a slumber party. We popped popcorn. We watched movies. We fixed one another's—"

Priscilla remembered the curls.

"Fixed one another's what?" said Felicity.

Priscilla swallowed hard. "I forget."

"Never mind," said Mr. Piper. "You've done a fine job of telling about a worthwhile activity. Take your seat."

"Mr. Piper!" said Felicity. "Priscilla told. Now she should take off her visual aid. Otherwise it might distract some of us when we try to do our work."

"Thank you for that reminder," said Mr. Piper. "Priscilla?"

Priscilla looked at Felicity.

Felicity smiled her snaky smile.

Priscilla looked at Mr. Piper.

"Cap?" Mr. Piper pointed to his head.

Priscilla chewed her lip. She could say no. But Mr. Piper wouldn't like that. And in the end she'd have to take it off, anyway.

Priscilla took a deep breath. "I need to tell one more thing before I take off the cap. At the slumber party what we fixed— We fixed my hair."

She slid off her cap.

Curls sprang out.

"Goodness!" said Mr. Piper.

"Gross!" said Jocko.

Felicity patted her own hair. "Curls have to be natural to look right."

"I didn't want curls," said Priscilla. "What I wanted was bounce. The Hi-5s gave me a body perm, but it didn't come out exactly right."

Ariel and Raheem started to giggle.

Mr. Piper gave them a stern look.

They stopped.

"Priscilla's hair didn't come out the way she wanted," said Mr. Piper. "But she's had a good learning experience."

Everyone nodded.

"It was brave of her to try something new," said Mr. Piper.

Priscilla felt herself glow. She felt as if she really were brave. "There's another new thing I'd like to try. I'd like to start a Hi-5 club in our school. We'd do community projects. We'd wear caps so that people who needed help could spot us."

"A school service group is a fine idea," said Mr. Piper. "What do others think?"

Julianne looked uncertain.

So did Henry.

"A club like that is all right for ordinary little people," said Felicity. "I'm a star. I have more important things to do."

Priscilla looked around. Kids who had looked interested didn't anymore. In a minute—

"*I'm* no star," said Jocko. "If we get to wear caps, I'll join Priscilla's club. As long as those caps are black and silver."

"Black and silver is okay with me," said Priscilla.

Mr. Piper smiled. "If you get three more classmates to join, you'll qualify as an official school club. I'll be happy to serve as your adviser. I'll even wear one of your caps."

"I'll join!" said Mary.

Raheem and Pam said, "We'll join, too!"

"Let's meet after school to make plans." Mr. Piper

stepped to the chalkboard. He wrote, "2:30 First meeting of"—

He turned. "What shall we call this club?"

Priscilla said, "Junior Hi-5s?"

"That sounds as if it's a junior high school club," said Raheem.

"Not Quite Hi-5s?" said Henry.

"That sounds as if it's for people who don't know what they're doing," said Mary.

"What about calling yourselves Young Hi-5s?" said Mr. Piper.

Priscilla didn't want to hurt Mr. Piper's feelings, but that name was *dull*.

"Pssst—I know what you can call your club," whispered Felicity. "Priscilla's *Non*stars. Priscilla's Little Nobodies. Priscilla's Faceless—"

Priscilla sat up straight. She blinked. "I have a name. I have the perfect name. How about—Ordinary Little People?"

Raheem and Ariel looked at each other.

"Cool name!" said Raheem.

"Great name!" said Ariel.

Mr. Piper said, "Priscilla, that's just excellent!"

Priscilla squirmed with pleasure. She watched Mr. Piper write the name on the board.

"Some *ordinary* people may be impressed," whispered Felicity. "This star is not."

Priscilla didn't care. Priscilla had her club.

Besides, she could tell by Felicity's scowl—impressed is just what Felicity was!

|2| Snow Day

Snow started to fall during social studies. One lazy flake drifted by Priscilla's classroom window. Then another. Then another. They landed on the giant willow tree and stuck.

Priscilla leaned sideways. "Pssst—Mary!"

Mary looked up from the map of Australia she was drawing.

Priscilla pointed.

Mary looked out the window. Her eyes got big. By recess snow had begun to stick to the playground and street. By early afternoon it was falling so hard Priscilla couldn't see the street from the classroom window. She could barely see the playground.

Mary leaned sideways. "Pssst!" She handed Priscilla a note.

Mary wore a cap just like Priscilla's. Black and silver. With letters that said OLP across the front.

Priscilla took the note and straightened her cap. She didn't need it to cover her hair anymore. The permanent had worn off before Christmas. Priscilla wore the cap now just to show she was a member. To show she was ready to help out. She liked it that Mr. Piper wore a cap, too.

Ordinary Little People had five members, including Priscilla. That was just enough to make OLP an official school club. There had been eleven members when the club started in October, but some dropped out. They quit because members had to do more than wear a cap and act important. Members had to collect bottles and cans, clean up the park, and do other hard work. But they had fun doing it. Especially Priscilla. Especially when Mr. Piper was around.

Priscilla opened Mary's note.

It said, "Snow day tomorrow!!!"

It said, "Sleds!!!"

It said, "Half Mile Hill!!!"

Priscilla could hardly sit still she was so excited. Half Mile Hill was the biggest hill in town. Or the second biggest. Batten Hill was taller and steeper. But Batten Hill was behind a high iron fence on private property. No one was allowed to sled there.

People *were* allowed to sled on Half Mile Hill. If enough snow fell, the hill got too slippery for cars. The police closed the road. Whoever wanted to sled on it, then, could.

Priscilla's favorite feeling all winter was the feeling of racing down that hill on her sled. Cold, tingly air rushed by her face. She plunged downward, hit the final bump, sailed into space, and . . . fell to earth, *thud*. Seconds passed before her stomach caught up with her.

You didn't have to live on Half Mile Road to sled

on the hill. You didn't have to get permission from anyone who did. You certainly didn't have to *pay* anyone who lived there. Even though one someone who lived there always tried to make you believe you did.

"Pssst, Olp-girl!"

Priscilla turned.

Felicity leaned forward across her desk. Felicity said "OLP" that way on purpose. To make it sound like a burp.

"I saw Mary's note," said Felicity. "If you two want to sled on my hill, you'll have to pay the admission fee. It's five dollars this year."

"There's no admission fee!" whispered Priscilla. "You know there isn't."

Felicity smiled a snaky smile. "The fee is seven dollars for Olp members. But there's a three-dollar discount if you quit the club first."

Felicity had been trying to get rid of Ordinary Little People from the day the club started. She talked Julianne into quitting. She told Paul and Nancy if they joined, they'd have to spend every weekend washing cars. Felicity didn't like OLP because its members got lots of attention. Priscilla, the club founder, got the most attention of all.

"Felicity?" said Mr. Piper. "Priscilla? Is there something you girls want to share with the rest of the class?"

Priscilla swallowed. "I was just saying—I was just asking—"

Felicity stood. "Priscilla said she hoped school would close early. I said I hoped not. I said you're a *great* teacher! I couldn't *stand* to miss even a minute of your class."

Mr. Piper looked doubtful. "Thank you for the compliment. But if this snow keeps up, Priscilla may get her wish. School *may* close early. If snow falls all night, school certainly will be canceled tomorrow. I wouldn't mind. I like sledding, too."

"Yeaaa!" shouted everyone.

Priscilla thought, Maybe Mr. Piper will come to Half Mile Hill. Maybe he'll watch me sled—

"Five dollars!" whispered Felicity. "Seven for Olp members!"

Priscilla whispered back, "No!"

"Raheem," said Mr. Piper. "What will you do tomorrow if it's a snow day?"

"My sister and I will build a snow fort," said Raheem. "We'll clobber anyone who tries to attack!"

"Ariel," said Mr. Piper. "What about you?"

Ariel stood. "My brother and I will track wild animals. We found bear tracks once. Right in our backyard."

"Bear tracks?" said Mr. Piper. "Here in town?"

Ariel shrugged. "The only other animal big enough to have made those tracks was my cat."

"I see," said Mr. Piper. "Mary, what will you do?"

Priscilla sat up straighter. She knew what Mary would say.

"I'll go sledding with Priscilla," said Mary. "On Half Mile Hill!"

"I'll go sledding, too!" said Lauren.

"I've been waiting for snow like this all winter!" Jocko turned his OLP cap backward. "I'll be sledding, too."

"Mr. Piper!" said Felicity.

Mr. Piper clapped for quiet. "Let's speak one at a time and only when called on. Felicity?"

Felicity stood. She fluffed her ruffles. She gave Priscilla a snaky smile.

Priscilla stiffened. There was nothing Felicity could do to stop her from sledding. Not one thing. But Priscilla felt nervous just the same.

"Well, Felicity," said Mr. Piper, "what are your plans?"

"I don't want to tell about plans," said Felicity. "I want to say that snow and ice might be fun for us kids. But for some people it means only trouble."

"Which people?" said Raheem.

Felicity clutched her hands in front of her chest. She made her eyes big and sad. "People who are old and need help shoveling their walks. People who are sick and need medicine from the drugstore. People who have babies and need stuff from the market—" Felicity paused to wipe a large, fat tear from her cheek.

Priscilla blinked. It wasn't like Felicity to think of other people.

"There, there." Mr. Piper offered her a tissue. He put a hand on her shoulder. "It's good of you to think of those in need. But don't worry. Those people can call the town hot line. Hot line volunteers will help."

"That's a relief." Felicity dried her tears. She started to sit, but then she didn't.

Uh-oh, thought Priscilla.

Felicity stood still and blinked as though she'd just gotten an idea. "*Heyyy*, isn't that what Priscilla's club is for? To help people in need?"

Priscilla's stomach turned to ice.

"Well, yes," said Mr. Piper. "I suppose you're right."

"So I guess all those people wearing OLP caps won't sled or have snowball fights tomorrow," said Felicity. "I guess they'll help at the hot line instead."

Mr. Piper turned to Priscilla. "What do you think, Priscilla? As your club adviser I must say it sounds like an excellent idea. Are you and the Ordinary Little People willing to give up your snow day to help those in need?"

"I'm not," said Jocko.

"Me neither!" said Mary. "I think we should help those needy people some other time."

Priscilla didn't know what to say. She thought of people too old to shovel their walks. She thought of people too sick to go to the store. She wanted to help. But the snow—the sledding—

Felicity sniffled. "If OLP doesn't help, all those needy people will suffer."

Mr. Piper looked at Priscilla. "Priscilla?"

Priscilla thought of racing down Half Mile Hill on her sled. She felt the cold, tingly air in her face. She felt the sled hit the bump and soar into space higher and higher. . . .

Priscilla sighed. "I'll help at the hot line. That's what Ordinary Little People is for."

"Bravo, Priscilla!" said Mr. Piper.

Felicity whispered, "Bravo, Olp-girl!"

Priscilla knew Felicity didn't mean "bravo."

Felicity meant, "Too bad for you!"

That night at dinner Priscilla said, "I'd be happy to shovel people's walks. Or go to the store for them. Or help with their babies. I just wish I had a choice."

"No one likes to be forced," said her father.

"Especially not by trickery," said her mother.

"Especially not by Felicity," said Eve. "She's such a snake."

Pow-wow growled under the table.

"Are all the Ordinary Little People going to help?" said Priscilla's father.

"Lauren is. And Anthony," said Priscilla. "Mary and Jocko said no. They quit the club. They said it wasn't turning out the way they expected. It wasn't enough fun."

Her mother turned to Eve. "Couldn't the Hi-5s help?"

"We'd like to help," said Eve. "But tomorrow we volunteer at the hospital."

For a minute everyone was silent.

Priscilla stared at the carrots scattered on her white plate. Carrots weren't what she saw. What she saw were sleds rocketing down a steep white slope. "Maybe if we start early enough tomorrow, we can finish in time to go sledding."

"That's the spirit!" said her mother. "Think positively."

"I'll call Lauren and Anthony after dinner," said Priscilla. "I'll tell them to bring their sleds just in case."

"Good idea!" said her father. "No matter how hard the problem, there's usually a solution."

"Maybe," said Eve. "But there's usually not a Felicity."

**S**now fell all night. In the morning, when Priscilla woke, it was still falling. The firehouse whistle blew to cancel school. Snow fell while Priscilla dressed, but it wasn't falling as hard as before.

Priscilla left for the hot line office right after breakfast. She wore her warmest parka, her tallest boots, and her Ordinary Little People cap. She dragged her sled behind her.

As she trudged along the sidewalk, the snow reached Priscilla's knees. In drifts it reached her waist. It was dry snow. Powdery snow. Perfect snow for sledding.

Priscilla blazed a trail up Lockwood Avenue. She blazed a trail down Weskum Woods Road. At the top of Half Mile Hill she stopped to catch her breath.

Snow lay deep and untouched on the hill.

Too deep to sled through, thought Priscilla.

Later that morning people would tramp it down. By noon the snow would be firmly packed and smooth. By afternoon it would be slick and fast.

As fast as an Olympic bobsled course, thought Priscilla.

"Hey, Olp-girl!" Felicity stepped out of her front door. She wore an all-in-one ski outfit. It was pink with a pattern of lavender snowflakes. It fit as tightly as skin from hood to foot. If it hadn't been for the ruffles on the cuffs of her pink gloves—and the ruffles on the tops of her pink boots—Felicity would have been ruffle free.

"Why are you stopping here?" Felicity hurried down her cleared front walk. "I've heard radio announcements: 'Dial HOT LINE for help. Volunteers are standing by.' Go on, Olp-girl. You'll be late. Shoo!"

"I'm taking a rest. I'll go in a minute," said Priscilla.

Felicity held out her arms and turned in place. "How do you like my outfit? It's for the 'Snowflake' number I do in dance class. I can wear it with long underwear for sledding, too."

Priscilla wasn't sure about the colors. She didn't

like the ruffles. But she did like the sleek way the suit fit. She shrugged. "It's nice, I guess."

"You bet it's nice!" Felicity fluffed her glove ruffles. "I'll look cosmic when I race downhill on my sled. Which reminds me. Why have you got your sled? You're not sledding today."

"I'm not sledding this morning," said Priscilla. "But later I might. If hot line work finishes early, I can come back here. I have my sled just in case."

Felicity stepped close to Priscilla. She nudged her in a friendly way. "Why don't you forget that hot line? You wouldn't have to help out at all, then. You could spend the whole day sledding on this." She waved her arm over the hill.

Priscilla gazed at the beautiful snow-covered slope. She thought, I *could* do that. I could stay right here and sled all day. . . .

"All you have to do," said Felicity, "is quit your ordinary little club—"

"No!" Priscilla started down the hill. "I said I'd help. That's what I'm going to do."

Priscilla was ashamed of herself for having thought of going back on her word. No Hi-5 would ever do that. No Ordinary Little Person should.

"Your ordinary little club is doomed!" Felicity yelled after her. "It's already lost two members. Find more fast, or Olp is through!"

Priscilla pulled her sled and pretended not to hear.

**T**en minutes later Priscilla arrived at the hot line building. She propped her sled in the hallway and went into the office.

People rushed in all directions.

Phones rang on every desk.

Lauren was already there.

She looked as though she'd rather be sledding.

Anthony tramped in right behind Priscilla.

He looked as though he'd rather be sledding, too.

"Lauren? Anthony?" Mrs. Batten, the hot line director, walked up to greet them. "Priscilla Robin? Are you the girl who started Ordinary Little People? Good for you!"

Priscilla dug her boot toe into the carpet and felt proud. She was glad she'd come to help. She was glad she hadn't stayed with Felicity on Half Mile Hill.

"We plan to keep the three of you very busy this morning," said Mrs. Batten.

"Just this morning?" said Priscilla. "What about this afternoon?"

"Mornings are always busy," said Mrs. Batten. "As a rule there's not much for volunteers to do in the afternoon."

"I see." Priscilla looked from Lauren to Anthony.

Anthony pumped the air with his fist.

Lauren whispered, "Yeaaa!"

Priscilla felt the tingle of cold air on her face. The sledding on Half Mile Hill would be good that morning. The sledding that afternoon would be great!

Priscilla's first job was to bring milk and bread to Mrs. Wilkins and her two-month-old twins.

Mrs. Wilkins held a baby in each arm. "My husband's away on a business trip. The twins and I couldn't have managed without your help. Thank you, Priscilla!"

Priscilla's second job was to shovel old Mr. Lewis's front walk.

Mr. Lewis stood at his door and watched. "There's nothing I like better than to shovel snow. But my doctor says I shouldn't do it."

The snow was light, but the front walk was long. It was nearly eleven o'clock when Priscilla finished. She looked at her work. The path she'd made was straight and clean.

"Ordinary Little People are fine snow shovelers!"

said Mr. Lewis. "I couldn't have done it better myself. Priscilla, thank you."

Priscilla returned to the hot line office.

Priscilla's third job was to fix soup and toast for an elderly lady, Mrs. King. She was sick in bed with a cold.

"This probably will be your last job." Mrs. Batten held the door as Priscilla started off. "It's nearly noon. The radio has stopped announcing our number, and lots of roads have been cleared."

Priscilla heated chicken soup in Mrs. King's microwave. She toasted bread and buttered it. She found a napkin, spoon, and tray and brought everything to Mrs. King's bedside.

"Aren't you thoughtful to help out like this!" said Mrs. King. "When I was your age, I spent snow days sledding on Half Mile Hill."

"I'm sledding there this afternoon," said Priscilla. She helped Mrs. King sit up in bed. "I like sledding a lot, but I like helping out, too."

It was true. While Priscilla carried groceries, shoveled snow, and fixed lunch, she hadn't wished she were sledding. She'd felt useful, grown up, proud. She bet Mr. Piper would have been proud of her, too.

But now that she was almost done, Priscilla couldn't wait to jump on her sled. She sat patiently while Mrs. King finished eating. She cleared the lunch tray and got ready to leave.

As Priscilla stepped out the front door, Mrs. King called to her, "Take one extra-fast sled ride for me!"

Priscilla started back to the hot line office. She took the long way by the bottom of Half Mile Hill. The snow on the hill was packed hard. The kids who'd been sledding there since early morning looked cold and tired. One after another they trudged past Priscilla on their way home.

Priscilla stamped her feet against the cold. This afternoon she, Lauren, and Anthony would have the hill all to themselves. They'd rocket down the hard packed snow. They'd reach the final bump, hit it, and—

"Hey, Olp-girl!"

Priscilla looked at the hilltop.

A pink and lavender figure took a running start and plunged downhill on her sled. "I hate to tell *yooou*"—Felicity zoomed over the snow toward Priscilla—"but you and your *Ooolp* friends are missing the best sledding of the *centuryyy!*"

Felicity's sled hit the bump. She flew into the air higher and higher—

She and the sled thudded to earth and coasted to

a stop right at Priscilla's feet. Felicity sat up. She pushed her pink goggles onto her forehead. "Prepare for the end, Olp-girl!"

Priscilla blinked. "What do you mean?"

"*You* may want to stay in your club after missing the sledding. Lauren and Anthony won't! No more members, no more club. No more wearing your cap around school and impersonating a star."

"We're not going to miss the sledding," said Priscilla. "Our jobs are done."

"What do you mean, *done*?" said Felicity.

For a moment it was so quiet Priscilla could hear the snow fall from a nearby tree. She heard wind in the tree's bare branches. She shrugged. "Mornings are busy at the hot line. In the afternoon there's not much for volunteers to do. I'm going to the office now to get my sled. Anthony, Lauren, and I are going to sled all afternoon."

"What if some needy person calls late?" said Felicity.

"The hot line director told us no one would," said Priscilla. "She told us once the snow stops, radio announcements stop. Calls stop, too."

"Calls stop, too . . ." Felicity let her voice trail off. She frowned as though she were trying to solve a puzzle.

Priscilla left her at the bottom of the hill. "See you very, very soon!"

**T**en minutes later Priscilla stepped into the hot line office.

People rushed around.

Every phone rang.

"Thank goodness you're back!" said Mrs. Batten. "Calls are pouring in from all over town."

"You mean, you still need helpers?" Priscilla hoped as hard as she could the answer would be no.

"I've sent Lauren out already. Anthony just left. You sit down and eat one of these sandwiches and then—" Mrs. Batten paused. "How do you get along with dogs?"

"I get along well," said Priscilla. "I have a dog. All the dogs I know like me."

"Wonderful!" said Mrs. Batten. "You can walk

a dog for a lady on Hearthstone Drive and then go
to the drugstore for a gentleman on Field Road. And
then—"

Priscilla's heart sank.

The hot line stayed busy all afternoon. Priscilla
barely had time to go to the bathroom. Lauren and
Anthony were just as busy as she was. They barely
had time to nod to Priscilla when they saw her in
the office. When they did nod, they looked mad.

Late that afternoon Priscilla returned to the office
from a snow-shoveling job. Lauren and Anthony
were waiting for her. The wall clock said four forty-
five. Mrs. Batten was turning off the office lights.

"Evening calls will go to the police station," said
Mrs. Batten.

Thank goodness! thought Priscilla. She and the
others could take at least a couple of sled rides before
dark.

"This was the busiest day I've ever seen!" Mrs.
Batten turned to smile at them. "You three Ordinary Little People did excellent work. No wonder

callers began to ask for you by name."

"By name?" said Lauren.

"They asked for me?" said Anthony.

Mrs. Batten nodded. "All three of you. All afternoon. Someone gave your names to the radio station. Someone asked the station to announce the hot

line phone number and your names every twenty minutes."

*Someone*? thought Priscilla. She knew just which someone.

Someone who wanted to keep them from sledding.

Someone who wanted to break up Ordinary Little People.

Someone whose initials were . . . Felicity Doll!

"A newspaper reporter even called," said Mrs. Batten. "He'd heard the radio announcements. He wanted to know who you three were."

Priscilla thought, If only I hadn't told Felicity, we could have been sledding all afternoon!

She was glad Lauren and Anthony didn't know. They already were mad enough.

"Come along," said Mrs. Batten. "I'll give you children a ride home."

"Thank you," said Anthony. "But we're not going home."

"We're going sledding," said Lauren.

Priscilla said, "On Half Mile Hill."

"Half Mile Hill?" Mrs. Batten looked startled.

"You can't sled there. Half Mile Hill has been open to traffic since midafternoon."

Priscilla looked at Lauren and Anthony.

They looked tired. They looked cold and fed up. Ready to quit Ordinary Little People was how they looked.

Priscilla couldn't stand it. OLP was a good club. It did good things. Now it was going to fall apart. All because of Felicity.

"I'll tell you what," said Mrs. Batten. "It's too late for sledding today, but bring your sleds to my house tomorrow. Bring your friends and classmates, too. We'll have a sledding party in honor of OLP!"

Priscilla looked at Lauren and Anthony.

Their faces looked the way she felt.

Their polite smiles said, Thank you.

Their glum eyes said, What a waste of time!

"How about it?" said Mrs. Batten.

Priscilla sighed. Mrs. Batten was trying to be nice, but she didn't understand about sledding. The hill at her house would be a bump in the ground compared with Half Mile Hill.

"Thank you," said Priscilla. "But it wouldn't be

the same. Half Mile Hill is the biggest hill in town.''

"It's the steepest and fastest," said Anthony.

Lauren nodded. "It's the best."

"The only hill that's bigger is the private one behind the iron fence," said Anthony.

"*Batten* Hill . . ." Priscilla let her voice trail off.

Mrs. Batten patted Priscilla's shoulder. She smiled at all three children. "Come tomorrow right after school. We'll have hot cider and sandwiches. I'll call the newspaper and get a photographer to take your picture. That kind of excitement could make OLP a very popular club!"

Lauren accepted a ride home from Mrs. Batten. So did Anthony.

Priscilla didn't. She said she'd rather walk.

"Even up Half Mile Hill?" said Mrs. Batten.

"Especially up Half Mile Hill!" said Priscilla. She started off.

Priscilla crossed the park. She reached Half Mile Hill and began to climb. Halfway to the top, just as Priscilla had expected, someone yelled at her.

"Hey, Olp-girl!"

Felicity stepped out her front door. She hurried to the end of her walk. "I didn't see you this afternoon. I guess the hot line was busier than you expected."

"It was very busy," said Priscilla. "Thanks to someone who spread our names all over town."

Felicity fluffed her glove ruffles. "I made one call. To the radio station."

Priscilla nodded. "That was enough."

"I guess Lauren and Anthony are pretty angry at you." Felicity smiled a snaky smile. "I guess they're fed up being members of your Olp club."

Priscilla shrugged. "They were upset. They were thinking of quitting. But not anymore."

"Why not?" said Felicity. "They missed the sledding. They spent the whole snow day doing ordinary little work."

"That's true," said Priscilla. "But those radio announcements made us sort of famous. Lauren and Anthony liked that. So did I. Tomorrow a newspaper photographer is going to take our picture. At a

sledding party in our honor." She paused. "On *Batten* Hill."

"No one sleds on Batten Hill," said Felicity. "It's private. No one."

"Lauren, Anthony, and I are going to sled there," said Priscilla. "The hot line director, Mrs. Batten—"

"*She* runs the hot line?" said Felicity.

"She told us to bring whoever we want," said Priscilla. "I'm inviting Mr. Piper. And guess what?"

Felicity narrowed her eyes. "What?"

Priscilla patted her shoulder. "I'm also inviting you!"

Felicity stared. "Why would you do that?"

"Because it's the right thing to do," said Priscilla. "Because I want you to join in the sledding. I want you to share the refreshments."

Felicity fluffed her glove ruffles. "I suppose I *could* make a special, star appearance."

Priscilla started to back away. "I especially want you to be a part of the nameless, faceless crowd that has to say, 'Ordinary Little People, hip-hip-hooray!' "

She turned and ran.

Felicity's snowball came close.

But by the time it hit, Priscilla had topped the hill. She was already running down the far side toward home.

3 | "Trees"

Marrch winds howled outside the Robins' house. Rain hammered the roof. Inside, Priscilla and her family ate dinner.

"Tomorrow Ordinary Little People decides what its next project should be," said Priscilla.

After the Batten Hill sledding party eleven new members had joined. Mary, Julianne, and Jocko rejoined. There were seventeen members in the club now. They'd elected Priscilla president.

"Lauren's calling tonight so we can talk about

ideas." Priscilla reached for a breadstick.

"If this storm lasts much longer," said her father, "OLP and Hi-5s will have enough projects to keep them busy all spring."

Priscilla swallowed a mouthful of stew. "What projects?"

Outside something crashed.

"Cleaning up fallen tree branches," said Eve.

"From this storm?" said Priscilla. "We could clean up glitter and gold paper stars, too."

Her parents looked puzzled.

"Felicity has pailfuls of the stuff," said Eve. "She gets little kids to carry the pails and scatter stars and glitter in her path."

"That must make quite a spectacle," said Priscilla's father.

"Felicity does have a flair for showmanship," said her mother.

Eve said, "Felicity has a flair for being a snake."

Something else crashed outside.

Pow-wow ran to the dining room window and barked.

"That was someone's trash can blowing over," said Priscilla's mother. "There'll be litter everywhere. What a mess."

"The way that wind is blowing," said her father, "we'll be lucky if branches and litter are all that come down tonight. That wind sounds strong enough to topple a tree."

Another something crashed.

"There goes another trash can!" said Eve.

The telephone rang.

"I'll get it." Priscilla pushed away from the table and ran to the front hall.

Pow-wow ran with her and barked.

Priscilla picked up the phone. "Quiet, Pow-wow. Hello?"

"This is a warning, Olp-girl!" said the caller. "Your Olp-head's getting too big for your Olp cap."

"Who is this?" said Priscilla. She knew exactly who it was.

"You may be club president," said the caller. "That doesn't make you a star."

"I never said I was a star," said Priscilla. "I never acted that way."

"I'm the star of the fourth grade!" said the caller. "The only star. Steal my spotlight one more time and you'll be sorry!"

"I'm already *sorry*," said Priscilla. "Sorry to be talking to *you*!" She slammed down the phone and hurried back to the dining room.

Pow-wow hurried, too.

"Was that Lauren?" said her mother.

Priscilla pulled out her chair and sat. "That was Felicity."

"Quick, get the snakebite kit!" said Eve.

"Hush," said their mother.

"What did Felicity want?" Their father reached for the pepper. "The homework assignment?"

"She wanted to warn me," said Priscilla. "She says I'm showing off. She says that being OLP president doesn't make me a star. She says to stop acting like one, or I'll be sorry."

"*Sorry?*" said her father. "What does that mean?"

"It means trouble," said Eve. "It means Priscilla

had better stay out of the spotlight. She'd better not attract any attention. Not until Felicity calms down."

"That'll be easy," said Priscilla. "I'm an ordinary little person. Not a star."

**P**riscilla woke up the next morning to find the rain had stopped. The wind had stopped. Birds twittered in the tree outside her window. Soggy trash and fallen branches lay on the lawn.

As she sat down to breakfast, Priscilla said, "I guess storm cleanup will be the new OLP project. I guess cleaning up this mess *could* take all spring."

"That should make Felicity happy," said Eve.

Their father looked up from his grapefruit. "Why is that?"

"Because," said Eve, "cleaning up messes is a totally *non*star, *non*spotlight kind of job."

"That's right," said Priscilla. She finished her breakfast, pulled on her jacket, and left for school.

**E**ven from a distance Priscilla could tell some-

thing had happened. Everyone was gathered on the
playground. Not just kids. Teachers, too. Even
Mrs. Goodfellow, the principal, was there.

Priscilla spotted Mary in the crowd. "What's going on?"

"It's the tree!" said Mary. "Look."

Priscilla looked. She saw sky. She saw people.

What she didn't see was the giant willow tree.

"Over there." Mary pointed.

Priscilla stood on her toes. She peered over kids' heads and between teachers' shoulders. "Oh, no!"

There it lay. On its side in the grass. The giant willow's roots stuck out every which way.

Priscilla stared.

That tree had stood on the playground for as long as she could remember. She had climbed it every spring. In summer she'd lain in its shade. Just last week she'd crouched behind it to hide from Felicity. That giant willow was as familiar as her house. She'd expected it would stand there forever.

The school bell rang.

"Come along, Priscilla!" called Mr. Piper.

Priscilla followed the teacher into school. She followed him into the classroom.

"Let's take our seats and settle down," said Mr. Piper.

Priscilla sighed and started for her desk.

"Remember, Olp-girl." Felicity grabbed Priscilla's sleeve. "No one but me stands in the spotlight."

"If you say so." Priscilla shrugged off Felicity's hand and took her seat. She didn't have the heart to worry about Felicity. She was too upset about the tree.

**A**ll morning long Priscilla stole glances out the window at the fallen tree. That afternoon she saw a work crew arrive.

The crew took out a chain saw. They sawed the tree into pieces. They loaded the pieces into a truck. The truck drove away. The crew left.

Now there was nothing to see but a hole in the ground. Not one twig was left. Not one leaf. Nothing to remind Priscilla of that old familiar tree.

"The giant willow gave us shade in summer and beauty in autumn," said Mr. Piper. "It sheltered squirrels in winter and was a nesting place for birds in spring. The birds and squirrels must miss it."

Everyone sighed.

Mr. Piper said, "I know I do."

Priscilla felt like crying. "Couldn't the school get a new tree, Mr. Piper? Couldn't the school buy a tree and plant it?"

Mr. Piper looked from Priscilla to the playground. He cocked his head and frowned. "It would have to be a much smaller tree. . . ."

He seemed to be thinking aloud.

"But young trees grow quickly. Before long it would be big enough for birds' nests and squirrel holes. For autumn beauty and summer shade . . ."

"You're showing off, Olp-girl," whispered Felicity. "Steal my spotlight, and you'll live to regret it!"

"What do others think of Priscilla's idea?" said Mr. Piper.

"School money should go for serious classroom things. Not trees," said Felicity.

"The school budget is tight," said Mr. Piper. "But Priscilla's idea is still a good one."

Julianne nodded.

So did Raheem.

Mr. Piper said, "Ordinary Little People is looking for a new project. What if OLP were to raise money for the tree?"

Priscilla couldn't believe her ears. She couldn't ask for a better project.

"Yeahhh!" said everyone.

Everyone but Felicity.

"OLP should clean up the mess on the ground," said Felicity. "They should pick up branches and trash instead."

No one listened.

"We could plant the new tree where the old one stood," said Mr. Piper. "We'd have a tree-planting program and invite the whole school."

"Oboy!" said everyone.

"We're grateful to you, Priscilla," said Mr. Piper.

"Yea, Priscilla!" Everyone clapped and cheered.

Priscilla blushed. She felt proud. She felt . . . "Uhfff!"

Someone kicked the back of her chair.

That same someone whispered, "I warned you! You'll be sorry, Olp-girl. Soon."

Priscilla and Ordinary Little People started earning tree money right away. They collected cans and bottles in the neighborhood that afternoon. The following week they held a bake sale. The following, they collected junk from people's attics, cellars, and garages. They sold it in a tag sale at the school parking lot.

By the beginning of April Ordinary Little People had earned enough money to buy a small cherry tree. On April 4 Mrs. Goodfellow announced the tree-planting program. It would be on April 23 at two o'clock. The whole school was invited. Parents, too. The official groundbreaker would be Priscilla

Robin, president of OLP. She would dig the first shovelful of dirt while everyone watched.

Priscilla walked out of school that day feeling as cheerful and springy as the afternoon. Her parents would take time off from work to come to the program. Eve would get excused from high school. They'd watch her dig while the whole school applauded.

Priscilla caught her breath. Mr. Piper would applaud, too!

Jocko ran by her fast. "Hey, Priscilla, you're famous!"

Amy biked past. "Hey, Priscilla, I bet you'll get your picture in the newspaper again!"

For Priscilla it was like being a star *and* an ordinary little person at the same time. She was so excited she could hardly wait for the day of the program. She skipped along the sidewalk.

"Hey, Olp-girl!" Felicity stepped from behind a hedge.

Priscilla stopped short.

"I warned you!" Felicity held her books in one

hand. In the other she held a pail of glitter, stars, and confetti. "I told you to stop impersonating a star. Now it's too late."

Lauren ran past them. "Hey, Priscilla, how's it feel to be a superstar?"

"Priscilla doesn't know!" yelled Felicity. "Priscilla's an amateur. I'm the real thing."

She turned to Priscilla. "I'll give you one more chance. First, give me the groundbreaker part. Second, take this pail and scatter glitter and stars in my path for one week. Otherwise—"

"You don't scare me." Priscilla tossed her head and left.

But Felicity did scare Priscilla. Felicity scared her a lot.

The following morning Mr. Piper said, "Let's talk about next week's tree-planting program."

"Mr. Piper!" said Felicity.

Priscilla stiffened.

"Yes, Felicity," said Mr. Piper. "What is it?"

Felicity stood. "I don't have a part in the program.

But I still want to make it the best program it can be."

"That's most unselfish of you," said Mr. Piper.

"It's true. I am unselfish," said Felicity. "Every genuine star is."

"We're all ears," said Mr. Piper. "How would you improve the program?"

Felicity fluffed her ruffles.

Priscilla held her breath.

"I'd have the groundbreaker recite a poem," said Felicity.

"Poem?" whispered Jocko.

"I hate poems!" whispered Ariel.

Priscilla relaxed a little. Reciting a poem wouldn't be so bad.

Mr. Piper said, "Did you have a particular poem in mind?"

Felicity nodded eagerly. She made her eyes wide and sincere. "I have in mind 'Trees,' by Joyce Kilmer."

"That's a lovely poem!" said Mr. Piper. "During lunch I'll find it in the library and make a copy."

"I just happen to have a copy." Felicity reached inside her desk for a paper. She stopped. "There's one problem. Priscilla isn't used to performing. We can't expect her to memorize this poem, recite it, *and* shovel. Only an experienced star could do all that."

Priscilla clutched the edge of her desk. So that was Felicity's plan! Felicity thought that having to shovel dirt *and* say lines would make Priscilla nervous. So nervous she'd quit the groundbreaker part.

Felicity said, "A star with stage experience might be able—"

"I'll memorize that poem!" said Priscilla. "I'll recite it. I'm good at memorizing things."

"As an experienced star, I doubt it," said Felicity. "I know how hard performing can be."

"Why not let Priscilla try the poem?" said Mr. Piper. "Then we'll see."

"Wel-ll." Felicity shrugged. "If Priscilla really thinks she can do it."

"I *know* I can do it! I *want* to do it." Priscilla was so angry her cheeks flamed. This was just like

Felicity. Trying to trick her out of being the groundbreaker. She snatched Felicity's copy of the poem. She shoved the poem into her notebook. She couldn't wait to tell her family how she hadn't been tricked.

"**Y**ou're reciting a poem, too?" Priscilla's father put down the evening newspaper.

"That's quite an honor!" Priscilla's mother put aside her file from work.

Pow-wow ran in circles and barked.

Only Eve looked doubtful. "This poem was *whose* idea?"

"It was Felicity's idea," said Priscilla. "Felicity thought reciting the poem would make me nervous. She thought I'd back out and she could be the groundbreaker."

Her father chuckled. "It looks as though her plan didn't work."

"Maybe it did. Maybe it didn't. What's the poem?" said Eve.

Priscilla pulled Felicity's copy out of her notebook. She stood very straight, cleared her throat, and said, " 'Trees,' by Joyce Kilmer."

"A lovely poem!" said her father.

"The perfect poem!" said her mother.

Eve shook her head. "I might have guessed."

Priscilla felt her stomach turn.

"You haven't read it, have you?" said Eve.

Priscilla shook her head.

Eve said, "You'd better read it now. Aloud."

Priscilla lifted the paper. She braced herself and read.

" 'I think that I shall never see . . .' "

She paused to swallow.

" '. . . a poem lovely as a tree.' "

She lowered the paper and glanced at her family. "That part was okay."

"Of course it was," said her father.

"It couldn't be sweeter," said her mother.

"Keep reading," said Eve.

Priscilla began where she'd left off.

" 'A tree whose hungry mouth is prest—' "

The phone rang.

"I'll get it." Priscilla's mother hurried to the front hall. "Wait until I get back to read the rest."

Priscilla didn't mind waiting. She was feeling better now. The poem might be a little corny, but it was okay.

Her mother came back into the living room. "That was Felicity. She wanted to know if you'd read the poem."

Priscilla stopped feeling better.

"She said to call her just as soon as you have."

"I'll bet she did," said Eve. "Read, Priscilla."

Priscilla started over from the beginning.

" 'I think that I shall never see

A poem lovely as a tree.

A tree whose hungry mouth is prest

Against the earth's sweet flowing—' "

Priscilla stopped.

"Go on," said her father.

Priscilla couldn't go on.

" 'Sweet flowing' what?" said her father.

Priscilla couldn't speak.

" 'Against the earth's sweet flowing *breast*!' " said her mother.

"Isn't that a lovely image?" said her father.

Eve shook her head. "Not if you're in fourth grade!"

*Breast.*

Priscilla couldn't stop looking at the word. She couldn't say "breast" in front of the whole school. She couldn't say it in front of her whole class. In front of Mr. Piper.

"If Priscilla recites that line, all the kids will laugh at her," said Eve.

Her father nodded. "I'd forgotten what fourth graders were like."

"Oh, dear," said her mother.

Eve shook her head. "You really have to hand it to Felicity."

Priscilla didn't say anything. Priscilla was frozen with fear.

At school the next day Priscilla tried not to think about the poem. She tried to concentrate on her math problems instead.

"Hey, Olp-girl," whispered Felicity. "You didn't call me back last night. Did you memorize that poem? Did you *read* it?"

Priscilla gripped her pencil harder and pretended not to hear.

"I guess you *did* read that poem," whispered Felicity. "I guess that's why you're shaking like one of the leaves on your spotlight-stealing tree."

Priscilla finished her long division problem. She

hoped it was right. She was having trouble concentrating.

Felicity went on. "You'd better give that groundbreaker part to someone who can recite 'Trees' without getting laughed at! You'd better give it to a star. Me."

"Felicity?" Mr. Piper turned from writing on the blackboard. "Are you sharing something with Priscilla that the whole class should hear?"

Felicity cleared her throat and stood. "I told Priscilla she ought to rehearse that poem. In front of the whole class. To make sure she knows her part."

Mr. Piper nodded. "We certainly do need to rehearse. We want Priscilla to feel comfortable in her role. Do you think you can learn the poem by tomorrow, Priscilla?"

Priscilla didn't know what to say. If she said no, Mr. Piper might take the poem away from her. If she said yes—

"Are you feeling uneasy about your part in the program?" said Mr. Piper. "Would you like a less demanding role?"

Priscilla hesitated.

"You'd better pick someone else, Mr. Piper," said Felicity. "Someone with star presence and stage experience. Priscilla doesn't have the nerve."

"I do so have the nerve!" The words seemed to leave Priscilla's mouth by themselves.

"That's the spirit!" said Mr. Piper. "Come to school tomorrow ready to rehearse."

Priscilla nodded. She took a deep breath and relaxed. Uhfff!

A kick to her chair reminded her. She might have stopped Felicity from taking her groundbreaker part. But she still hadn't solved the big problem. She still had to find a way, before tomorrow's rehearsal, to make "breast" sound okay.

Priscilla worried about the rehearsal all that afternoon. She worried about it that night at dinner.

"Maybe your classmates are more mature than you think," said her mother. "Maybe they won't laugh."

"Maybe Pow-wow can fly!" said Eve.

"Here's my advice," said Priscilla's father. "Cough when you say the 'sweet flowing' part. Or mumble so that no one hears."

Priscilla slumped in her chair. "Mr. Piper's always telling us to speak up! If I mumble, he'll make me repeat that line. Over and over. Loud and clear."

"What you need is a diversion," said her mother.

"What's a diversion?" said Priscilla.

"Something to take people's attention off you," said her father.

"Priscilla would need a volcano eruption!" said Eve. "Or an avalanche."

Her parents laughed.

Priscilla didn't.

Priscilla was busy thinking. A diversion . . . Something to take people's attention . . .

Priscilla blinked.

The biggest diversion her school had—the biggest diversion Priscilla knew of anywhere—was a curly-haired, ruffle-wearing snake.

**A**t school the next day Mr. Piper said, "Rehearsal

time! Priscilla, come to the front of the room and let us hear you recite 'Trees.' "

Priscilla started to get up.

Someone kicked the back of her chair. The same someone softly snickered.

"Is there anything wrong, Priscilla?" said Mr. Piper. "Have you changed your mind about reciting in the program?"

Priscilla stood. "I haven't changed my mind. I've thought of a way to make the program better."

"Another improvement?" said Mr. Piper. "Tell us your idea."

Priscilla took a deep breath. "We don't have stars in Ordinary Little People. We think one person's as important as another."

"I couldn't agree more," said Mr. Piper.

"I don't want to stand up alone and act important," said Priscilla. "The more people who have parts in the ceremony, the better."

"Priscilla makes a good point," said Mr. Piper. "Doesn't she, class?"

"Ye-es," said everyone.

Priscilla said, "I thought that while I recite the poem, someone could do a dance."

"What sort of dance?" said Mr. Piper.

Priscilla glanced at Felicity. "A tree dance."

"Excellent idea!" said Mr. Piper. "Do we have a volunteer?"

Priscilla said, "There's someone in this class who's already played a tree in a dance recital."

"You mean Felicity?" said Mr. Piper.

Priscilla shrugged. "Felicity has a tree costume. She knows how to dance the part."

"Class," said Mr. Piper. "What do you think of the idea?"

"Goo-ood," said everyone.

"Felicity, what do you say?"

Felicity scrambled to her feet. "I know how to dance 'The Beauteous Autumn Tree.' I don't know how to dance 'The Ordinary Little Tree Gets Planted.'"

"But you have imagination," said Mr. Piper. "You have the poem's lovely words to guide you. Come up front, both of you. We'll give it a run-through."

Priscilla stood to one side and began. " 'Trees,' by Joyce Kilmer . . ."

Felicity took center stage. She gave Priscilla a dirty look, but she leaped and twirled.

When Priscilla got to the "sweet flowing" part, Felicity shot the class a "Laugh and you're doomed" glare.

"Happy face, Felicity! You're the spring tree," said Mr. Piper.

Kids wanted to laugh. Kids tried to laugh. But to Priscilla's relief, as long as they were in the classroom, no one dared.

The day of the program was sunny and warm. Priscilla stood on the playground beside the new cherry tree. The tree's roots were tied with burlap. Its leaves fluttered in the breeze.

Mrs. Goodfellow and Mr. Piper stood on the tree's other side. Felicity stood beside them in her shimmery leaf tutu and glitter-dusted hair. Her hands were closed in tight fists. She gave Priscilla a dirty look. She turned to the audience then and smiled her "I'm a Star" smile.

Priscilla straightened her OLP cap. She went over the program in her head.

Mrs. Goodfellow would introduce her. She'd dig one shovelful of dirt and give the shovel to one of the school groundskeepers. Then she'd recite "Trees."

While Priscilla recited, Felicity would dance. By the time they finished, the groundskeepers would have finished digging the deep, wide hole and planting the tree.

Priscilla looked out at the huge audience of parents, teachers, and children. They stood in a semicircle and waited for the ceremony to begin.

She spotted her mother and father.

They waved to her.

She spotted Eve.

Eve gave her a thumbs-up sign.

She spotted Jocko, Ariel, and Raheem.

They pointed to her and started to snicker. Ariel mouthed the word *breast*. Jocko cupped his hands over his chest and pranced around. Raheem pursed his lips, bent double, and pretended to suck the earth. The three of them laughed so hard they fell down.

Priscilla chewed her lip. During rehearsals everyone had been too scared to laugh. Out here on the playground no one was a bit scared. All Priscilla's classmates were just waiting to roar. Priscilla couldn't think of any way to stop them.

She looked at Felicity.

Not even she would be a big enough diversion today.

"Parents, students, teachers, and friends"—Mrs. Goodfellow stepped forward—"this happy occasion was made possible by Ordinary Little People of grade four. The president of that club, Priscilla Robin, will break ground for our new tree."

"*Yeaaa!*" Everyone cheered.

Priscilla picked up the shovel. She stuck it in the ground and lifted a big clump of grass and dirt.

Everyone clapped.

Priscilla handed the shovel to a groundskeeper.

Mrs. Goodfellow said, "Priscilla will recite a

poem. Her classmate Felicity Doll will do an inter-
pretive dance."

Felicity stepped forward.

Priscilla cleared her throat and began. " 'Trees,'
by Joyce Kilmer.

" 'I think that I shall never see . . .' "

Felicity stood on her toes. She turned in place.

" 'A poem lovely as a tree . . .' "

Felicity opened her arms and made a deep curtsy to the little tree.

"Ahhhh," said the audience.

" 'A tree whose hungry mouth is prest . . .' "

Felicity ran in a circle around the tree.

Priscilla braced herself. " 'Against the earth's sweet flowing . . .' "

Felicity threw up her arms and opened her fists. . . .

"Oooh!" said everyone as glitter rained on them.

"Ahhh!" said everyone as gold stars fell.

" '. . . breast,' " said Priscilla.

No one laughed. No one heard.

Everyone was ooohing and ahhhing too much.

**A**fterward Priscilla's family hurried over to congratulate her.

"You recited so well!" said her mother.

"You didn't make one mistake!" said her father.

Eve said, "You handled that shovel pretty well, too."

Priscilla touched the new little tree. She thought

of the giant willow. She felt sad. But happy, too.

She took off her cap and wiped her forehead.

She also felt relieved. "Felicity had the 'sweet flowing' part worked out pretty well," she said. "I guess she really is a star."

They all looked across the grass at Felicity.

People crowded around congratulating her.

Her uncle pointed a videocam at her.

Her parents snapped pictures.

"It was good to see you and Felicity work together for a change," said her mother.

"You got your tree planting," said her father. "Felicity got her spotlight. Maybe the two of you can start to cooperate."

Priscilla looked at Eve.

Eve rolled her eyes.

Priscilla shrugged. "I could try. *Hey, Felicity!*"

Felicity turned. She caught sight of Priscilla.

Priscilla gave her the thumbs-up sign. "We did it!"

"If you have a message for me, ordinary little person, put it in my fan mail." Felicity fluffed her tutu and turned away.

Priscilla looked at her family and grinned.

Her father shook his head.

Her mother and Eve giggled.

"I think that I shall never see a tree as snaky as Felicity," said Priscilla.

"Hush," said her mother. "You'll hurt her feelings."

But Felicity's feelings weren't hurt.

Felicity didn't hear.

Felicity was much too busy posing for pictures.

# 4 OLP Forever

That May afternoon the warm classroom made Priscilla sleepy. The OLP cap made her head sweat. She sat at her desk and daydreamed. About the last day of school. About summer vacation. About losing Mr. Piper as her teacher.

Priscilla wiped her forehead. She wondered if Mr. Piper ever thought of graduating from fourth grade to teach fifth.

"Remember, class," Mr. Piper was saying, "Ordinary Little People has an important meeting right after school. Members, keep your seats. Anyone who wants to join, stay put, too. OLP is open to everyone in the fourth grade."

"Some club!" whispered Felicity.

Priscilla fanned herself with her cap and tried not to listen.

"A real club says some people can join and some can't," whispered Felicity. "A real club says some people are good enough and some people aren't. What kind of club lets in everyone? A losers' club, that's what kind. A club this star would never join."

"We don't need stars," said Priscilla. "We need ordinary people who want to help."

The bell rang.

Kids who weren't Ordinary Little People gathered their books. They started for the door.

"Let me out of here! I'm allergic to ordinary *anything*." Felicity led the way.

Priscilla didn't care. Felicity was jealous because Ordinary Little People was popular. She was jealous because Priscilla was president.

Priscilla kept her seat.

So did Mary, Jocko, and Lauren.

So did more than half the class.

OLP members from the other fourth grades started to file in. Five members, ten, fourteen . . .

"If one more student joins this club"—Mr. Piper smiled at Priscilla—"we're going to have to meet in the auditorium."

Priscilla knew Mr. Piper was joking. But what he said was true. After the tree-planting program, Ordinary Little People had gotten to be more popular than ever. Wherever Priscilla looked in the fourth grade, she saw black-and-silver OLP caps. Lately some third and fifth graders had asked if they could be members. Even some sixth graders wanted to join.

Not everyone liked that idea.

"Let's begin," said Mr. Piper. "Mary, should we open OLP to students from other grades?"

"OLP is getting too big," said Mary. "If we don't watch out, everyone in the school will join."

Jocko said, "Third graders would turn OLP into a baby club."

Lauren said, "Fifth and sixth graders would boss us around and take over."

"OLP should be for fourth graders only," said Julianne. "We're the ones who made it popular. It was our idea."

"It was Priscilla's idea," said Mr. Piper. "Let's hear from her."

Priscilla blushed. But she wasn't sure what to say. Everything the others were nervous about was true. Bigger kids would try to boss. Younger kids would act, well, younger. But the whole idea of Ordinary Little People was to help out. "The more people we have as members," said Priscilla, "the more people there are to work on projects."

"That's my feeling," said Mr. Piper. "Let's vote."

"If you want fifth and sixth graders to order us around, vote yes," said Jocko.

"If you want to baby-sit for a bunch of little kids, vote yes," said Julianne.

Mr. Piper said, "All those in favor of opening Ordinary Little People to students from all grades?"

Priscilla raised her hand.

So did Anthony.

So did Lauren.

So did four others.

Mr. Piper said, "All those opposed?"

Julianne, Jocko, and Mary raised their hands.

So did everyone else.

"The motion to open OLP to other grades is

defeated," said Mr. Piper. "Let's move on to new business. Who has an idea for what we should do with the money in our treasury?"

"Let's have a party," said William.

"Party!" said Bethany.

Henry said, "Party!"

"I mean," said Mr. Piper, "to what good cause should we contribute the money?"

"Can't we have a party, pleeease?" said Jason.

"Please, please, *pleeease*?" said Julianne.

Mr. Piper looked from one to the other. He scratched his head, and then he smiled. "You OLPs worked hard all year. You helped the community in lots of ways. I suppose we could use a little money for a party. We can invite everyone in the fourth grade."

"Not *everyone*," said Lauren. "Ordinary Little People, only."

"We're the ones who earned the money," said Jocko.

"We're the ones who worked hard," said Patty. "Right, Priscilla?"

Priscilla shifted in her chair. Members were saying things that sounded sort of selfish. And familiar. They reminded her of Felicity.

Priscilla shrugged. "What's the difference? Ordinary Little People isn't a private club. It's open to everyone. Any fourth grader who wants to come to the party can say, 'Starting today, I'm a member,' and come."

For a minute no one said anything.

Everyone looked at one another.

Bethany raised her hand. "I move we make Ordinary Little People a private club."

"Private?" said Priscilla.

"Good idea!" said Jason.

Mr. Piper frowned. "Girls and boys, I want you to think carefully about this. I can't stop you from doing it. But I can tell you it's a very bad idea."

"No one can join unless we vote that person in," said Julianne.

"We can keep out riffraff," said Jocko. "It sounds good to me."

"Ordinary Little People is supposed to help others," said Mr. Piper. "You're supposed to make others feel good. If someone wants to join and you vote no, how will that person feel?"

"Like a loser!" Jason grinned.

"Like a nobody!" Ariel grinned, too.

Mr. Piper looked stern. "That person's hurt feelings will be your doing. Ordinary Little People's doing. Remember that, and let's vote."

That night at dinner Priscilla told her family the news. "As of today, Ordinary Little People is a private club."

"Private?" said Eve.

Priscilla nodded. "To get in, you have to have one member nominate you. You have to have another member second you. You have to have at least half the members vote for you."

"That's as hard as getting into the yacht club," said her father.

"Harder," said her mother. "If you keep that up, no one will want to join."

"That's the funny thing." Priscilla speared a tomato slice. "The news got out, and right away kids who'd always thought Ordinary Little People was a waste of time wanted to be members. If you're in OLP now, people think you're special. They envy you. They treat you like a—like a—"

"*Star?*" said Eve.

Under the table Pow-wow growled.

"That's not what I was going to say," said Priscilla. Even though *star* is exactly what she'd been thinking.

Some OLP members had started acting stuck up. As if being in OLP made them better than other kids. Priscilla had even caught herself showing off a little about being the club president.

That's what had made her uneasy at the meeting. Ordinary Little People was acting like Felicity!

"A star club sounds like bad news to me," said Priscilla's father.

"Ordinary Little People isn't turning into a club for stars!" said Priscilla. "I've told people that I'll nominate anyone who wants to join. I'll second anyone who needs seconding. I'll vote yes for anyone who gets nominated. Anyone."

"Even if that anyone is Felicity?" said Eve.

*Felicity?* For a second Priscilla felt nervous. Until she remembered what Felicity had said. "Felicity would never join OLP. Felicity's allergic to ordinary anything. Ordinary *people* especially."

Everyone went back to eating.


The next morning Priscilla rode her bike to school. She turned left into the parking lot. Birds hopped along the pavement, looking for crumbs. Priscilla coasted past them to the bike rack.

"Priscilla! My oldest, dearest friend!"

Priscilla looked up. She nearly fell off her bike.

Hurrying toward her across the playground was Felicity.

"I've got breakfast muffins to share with you!" Felicity held out a white paper bag. "They're fresh from the bakery. Which do you want, blueberry or corn?"

Priscilla stared at the bag. She stared at Felicity.

Felicity wore a white blouse and a candy-striped jumper. Exactly like the ones hospital volunteers wore. Except that Felicity's had ruffles.

Felicity smoothed the jumper. "This outfit is to remind others that it's good to help out. When I'm old enough, I may even volunteer."

Priscilla blinked. "But you said no star ever volunteers."

Felicity draped an arm around Priscilla's shoulders. She jiggled Priscilla in a long-lost-friend kind of way. "Priscilla, Priscilla, *Priscilla!*"

Priscilla was too startled to pull away.

"Is this a new blouse?" said Felicity. "It's *verrry* pretty. Let's eat our muffins and have a little talk."

Priscilla bit into the corn muffin. Corn was her favorite. She chewed and swallowed. "Why are you acting so nice? If you want something, just ask me."

Felicity dropped her arm. "I want to join Olp. I want you to nominate me at the meeting next week. I want you to vote for me. The way you said you'd nominate and vote for anyone who wanted to join."

Priscilla swallowed so hard she choked. "I thought you didn't have time for Ordinary Little People. I thought OLP wasn't the club for a star."

Felicity rolled her eyes. "That was before! You've made Olp a private club now. You've made it exclusive. Of course I'll join."

Priscilla shook her head. "You can't! I won't let you—"

"You said you'd nominate anyone who asked. I'm asking." Felicity crossed her arms and narrowed her eyes. "Are you going to go back on your word? Or are you going to nominate me?"

Priscilla hesitated. Whatever she did would be wrong. "You wouldn't like being an Ordinary Little Person. We do helping things. Not star stuff."

Felicity nudged her. "Vote me in, and I'll change all that."

"No!" said Priscilla.

"I'll get us club membership rings," said Felicity. "I'll get us club T-shirts. I'll get us club jackets—"

"We don't need those things," said Priscilla. "That's not what Ordinary Little People is about."

The first bell rang.

"That's what it *should* be about." Felicity swallowed the last of her blueberry muffin. She brushed crumbs from her fingers. "When I join, it will be."

Priscilla watched Felicity hurry into school.

*Felicity in OLP.*

Birds hopped around Priscilla's feet. They pecked at muffin crumbs in the spot where Felicity had stood.

Priscilla looked down at them. She looked at the half-eaten corn muffin in her hand. She broke it in pieces and tossed the pieces to them.

*Felicity in OLP.*

What a sickening idea!

**P**riscilla worried all week about how to save OLP. She worried while she sat at her desk at school.

"Priscilla, are you with us? Please answer problem number six."

She worried while she played catch with Eve.

"Wake up, Priscilla! That one was right to you."

The day before Ordinary Little People was to meet, Lauren and Anthony came to her house.

"You could keep Felicity from getting voted in," said Lauren.

"Kids may like Felicity's ideas about rings and jackets. But you're still president," said Anthony.

"If you say, 'Don't vote for Felicity,' " said Lauren, "no one will."

Priscilla heard their voices in her sleep that night.

*You can keep Felicity out. . . .*

*If you say so, no one will vote for her. . . .*

Priscilla tossed and turned so much that Pow-wow went downstairs to sleep.

The next morning Priscilla woke up feeling jittery. On the way to school she still didn't know what to do. Should she nominate Felicity and ruin Ordinary Little People? Should she *not* nominate Felicity and go against everything the club stood for?

A gust of wind blew down the street. It bent the June flowers sideways. It took off Priscilla's OLP cap—almost.

Priscilla jammed her cap down on her head and made up her mind. She wouldn't nominate Felicity. She'd vote no if someone else did. It would serve Felicity right.

Priscilla crossed Lemon Street. The wind was still gusting. The little boy in front of her stumbled and dropped his books. His papers blew everywhere. He looked as though he was going to cry.

Priscilla helped him gather the papers. She helped him dust off his knees and books.

"Thanks." The little boy clutched his things.

"You OLP guys are great!"

Priscilla felt proud as she finished the walk to school. She felt proud as she opened the door and stepped into the hall. She *would* nominate Felicity. It was the right thing to do. Besides, one person couldn't change a whole club—

Priscilla stopped walking. She stared down the hall.

Felicity stood by the classroom door. She held a rubber stamp and an ink pad. She grabbed the hand of each OLP member who passed and stamped it. "Vote me into OLP. I'll turn you into stars. Vote for me. I'll make sure we have lots of parties. Vote for me. I'll make sure we spend OLP money on us."

Members were listening. Members were letting her stamp them. Members were nodding and saying, "Oboy!"

Priscilla hurried up. "You can't promise any of that stuff, Felicity! You aren't even a member."

"But I'm going to be." Felicity stamped Bethany's hand. She gave Priscilla a snaky smile. "Because you're going to nominate me. Aren't you, Priscilla?"

Bethany and Henry looked at Priscilla.

Priscilla shifted from one foot to the other.

"You said Olp should be open to everyone. You made a promise. You can't go back on your word."

Bethany and Henry waited to hear what Priscilla would say.

"Wel-ll . . ." said Priscilla.

Felicity grabbed Priscilla's hand. She stamped it.

"Hey!" Priscilla pulled away. She stared at the gold imprint on her skin.

"It's glittery. It's indelible." Felicity re-inked her stamp and smiled her snaky smile. "It's the perfect reminder of me."

**O**rdinary Little People met in the cafeteria that afternoon.

"Some of you want to nominate new members,"
said Mr. Piper. "Lauren?"

Lauren said, "I nominate Josie."

Josie was voted in.

"Jocko?" said Mr. Piper. "Did you have a nomi-
nee?"

"I nominate Calvin," said Jocko.

Mary raised her hand. "I say, vote no on Calvin. He hits."

"He hit *you* because you called him Elephant Ears," said Jocko.

"Let's understand," said Mr. Piper. "Mary will not make remarks about Calvin's appearance, and Calvin will not hit anyone."

Calvin was voted in.

Mr. Piper turned to Priscilla. "A little bird told me that you have someone to nominate."

Priscilla frowned. She'd bet it hadn't been a little bird. She'd bet it had been a curly haired, ruffle-wearing snake.

"Priscilla?" said Mr. Piper.

"No, Mr. Piper. There's no one . . ." Priscilla let her voice trail off. She stared across the room.

Felicity gazed through the cafeteria window at her. She dabbed her eyes with a handkerchief. She mouthed, "Pleeease?"

Priscilla knew it was a trick. She knew Felicity's tears were phony tears. She knew the minute Felicity was voted into Ordinary Little People, she'd put away that handkerchief. She'd go back to acting like a snake.

*Pleeease?*

But knowing those things didn't change the facts. Priscilla had said OLP should be open to everyone. If she kept Felicity out, she'd be a snake, too.

"Priscilla?" said Mr. Piper.

Priscilla remembered Felicity's slogan: All for me and me for myself!

She remembered the Hi-5 slogan: One for all and all for one!

"Don't do it!" whispered Lauren.

"Don't let her wreck OLP!" whispered Anthony.

Priscilla looked at the teacher and sighed. "I nominate Felicity."

That night Priscilla's parents tried to cheer her up.

"You made a tough decision but a good one," said her father.

"You feel bad now, but nominating Felicity was the right thing to do," said her mother.

"How can you say that?" said Eve. "Felicity will take over. That club will never do another useful thing."

"One person can't change a whole club," said their mother.

"She can if that person is Felicity," said Eve.

Priscilla picked at her green beans. "Maybe not. You never know . . ."

But Priscilla did know. Priscilla always knew when it came to Felicity.

OLP met the following week.

"Who has new business?" said Mr. Piper.

Felicity raised her hand. "I do! Lots."

The first thing Felicity called for was fewer new members. "We only want kids with star quality," said Felicity.

"No!" said Priscilla.

All but five kids voted yes.

The second thing Felicity called for was fewer "helping" projects. "We're kids. We should be having fun."

"No!" said Priscilla.

All but four kids voted yes.

The third thing Felicity called for was a new club name. "There's nothing *ordinary* about us. There's nothing *little* about us. We're the most important kids in the fourth grade."

Anthony whispered, "Stop her, Priscilla!"

Lauren whispered, "Do something!"

"We have a new, improved club," said Felicity. "We need a new, improved name, too."

"No!" Priscilla couldn't stand it.

"Let's hear Felicity out," said Mr. Piper. "What name did you have in mind?"

"The perfect name." Felicity fluffed her ruffles. "Stars 'R' Us!"

"Good heavens," said Priscilla's mother that night at dinner. "What did Mr. Piper say to that?"

"He said, 'Let's think about it,' " said Priscilla. "He said we should vote on it at the final meeting."

"It'll be final in more ways than one," said Eve.

Priscilla nodded. "It's the last meeting of the year.

It'll be the last meeting of Ordinary Little People, too. Unless I get kids to vote with me against Felicity."

"It sounds like a regular showdown," said her mother.

"Stars 'R' Us?" Priscilla's father shook his head.

"Snakes 'R' Us would be more like it," said Eve.

Priscilla slumped in her chair. "That's what Anthony said."

Pow-wow scrambled to his feet. He rested his chin on Priscilla's lap and looked at her. He whimpered.

"I don't understand," said Priscilla's mother. "Why doesn't Mr. Piper tell Felicity no?"

Priscilla stroked Pow-wow's head and sighed. "Mr. Piper says the club's a democracy. He says he can only advise. In the end the club's whatever members want it to be."

"That sounds fair," said Priscilla's father.

"It's too fair," said Eve. "Mr. Piper doesn't know Felicity the way we do."

Priscilla's mother said, "Talk to Mr. Piper. Tell him what Felicity's up to."

"He'll think I'm jealous," said Priscilla. "Maybe I am jealous. But I'll try."

**P**riscilla put off trying for one day. Two days. A week.

On the morning of the meeting she couldn't put it off any longer. She left for school early. As she walked, she rehearsed what she would say:

"OLP should go back to being a club that helps people. It should stop having so many parties and leaving people out."

I won't blame Felicity, thought Priscilla. I won't say one word about Felicity.

She reached her classroom and opened the door.

"Good morning, Priscilla. You're here early." Mr. Piper was at his desk, alone. "Was there something you wanted to see me about?"

"Felicity's ruining OLP!" said Priscilla. All the things she'd planned not to say poured out.

Mr. Piper waited until she finished. "Felicity does have some unusal ideas. But let's think this through. Is it *all* Felicity's fault?"

Priscilla chewed her lip. She had to admit it wasn't. Felicity wasn't the one who'd voted to keep out kids from other grades. Felicity wasn't the one who'd made the club private. Priscilla didn't know why, but OLP had been going downhill even before Felicity joined.

Mr. Piper came around his desk. He put a hand on Priscilla's shoulder. "It's the end of the school year. Everyone's tired. OLP members are more interested in having fun than helping out. That may be a little selfish, but it's understandable. We all act selfish from time to time."

Priscilla thought of how she'd wanted to keep Felicity out of the club. That would have been selfish. She thought of how much she liked being OLP president. Not because of helping. But because people looked up to her and were impressed. That was selfish, too.

Priscilla looked at Mr. Piper. "The whole club

will change if we call it Stars 'R' Us. Can't you stop kids from doing it?"

"I'm just the adviser," said Mr. Piper. "You're the members. It's up to you."

Priscilla sighed. She couldn't think of anything else to say.

Sun shone through the classroom windows. A breeze sent the curtain cord tapping against the window frame. Outside, a songbird sang in the OLP cherry tree.

Priscilla watched the tree's branches dip on the breeze and rise. She felt the same sad way she had when the giant willow was carted off.

Felicity wore her CLAP! I'M A SUPER ☆ T-shirt that day.

Before the meeting she gathered all the members around her. "Vote for the new name, and this will be our official Stars 'R' Us T-shirt. Our club colors will be gold and pink. We'll have caps, jackets, and rings that say Stars 'R' Us."

Priscilla stood by the cafeteria's open window. She watched Felicity hand printed sheets to Jocko, Ariel, Mary, and the other OLP members.

"I've written an official club song. Everyone should learn it," said Felicity. "Here's the official Stars 'R' Us dress code. Here's the *Stars 'R' Us Hand-*

*book* with the do's and don't's of being a star."

"Why do we need all these things?" said Julianne.

Jason flipped through the handbook. "Why do we have to follow so many rules?"

"Because we're stars," said Felicity. "People are supposed to look up to us. We have to make sure they do."

"Wow!" said Mary. "I thought people were stars or they weren't. I didn't know being a star took work."

"I've been a star all my life." Felicity fluffed her ruffles. "You can trust me on this."

Priscilla turned to stare out the window. She couldn't stand it. There had to be a way to stop Felicity. There had to be a way to keep Ordinary Little People from turning into Stars 'R' Us.

Outside on the playground the cherry tree swayed with the breeze. Its branches dipped and rose.

The same breeze cooled Priscilla's cheeks.

That tree stood on the playground because of OLP. She could be proud of that. When the giant willow was carted away, OLP hadn't cried about it. They'd raised money and gotten the cherry tree to replace it.

Mr. Piper arrived. "Let's begin the meeting."

Kids took their seats.

The shadow of an idea flickered across Priscilla's mind. Maybe she'd been trying to do the wrong thing. Maybe instead of stopping Felicity—

"We have a motion on the table to change the name of Ordinary Little People to Stars 'R' Us," said Mr. Piper. "Does anyone second this motion?"

Priscilla took one last look at the cherry tree. She got to her feet. "I second Felicity's motion."

Mr. Piper looked startled.

Lauren looked startled.

The person who looked most startled of all was Felicity.

"Our club doesn't help ordinary people anymore," said Priscilla. "It doesn't have ordinary people as members. Felicity's right. It shouldn't be called Ordinary Little People. Not now. We might as well call it Stars 'R' Us."

Priscilla sat.

"A motion to change the name has been made and seconded," said Mr. Piper. "All those in favor?"

Everyone but Anthony and Lauren raised their hands.

Priscilla raised hers straight and high.

"All those opposed?" said Mr. Piper.

Lauren raised her hand.

Anthony raised his.

"The motion passes," said Mr. Piper. "The club is now called Stars 'R' Us."

"All *riiight*!" said Raheem.

"Now that we have a new, improved name, we need a new, improved president," said Felicity.

"No way!" said Anthony.

"Priscilla's president. We elected her!" said Lauren.

Priscilla stood again. "I resign as president. I resign from the club."

"Priscilla!" said Anthony.

"Stars 'R' Us isn't my kind of club," said Priscilla. "Maybe I'll start a new club."

"What kind of club?" said Julianne.

"One that helps people," said Priscilla. "One that does community projects."

"One that has only one member!" said Felicity.

"Who are you going to let join?" said Henry.

"It'll be open to everyone," said Priscilla. "No matter what grade a person's in. All you have to do is be willing to help."

Ariel and Raheem looked at each other.

Mary said, "What are you going to call this club?"

"I don't know . . ." Priscilla blinked. "Yes, I do. I'll call it Ordinary Little People."

"You can't do that!" said Felicity. "That's stealing. Mr. Piper, tell Priscilla she can't use that name. It belongs to us."

"It did belong to you," said Mr. Piper. "It doesn't now. You just voted it away. Priscilla has every right to use it if she wants."

Jocko said, "What are your club's colors going to be?"

"Colors?" Priscilla took off her cap and scratched her head. "I haven't thought about colors."

"What about silver and black?" said Jocko.

Priscilla shrugged. "That's okay with me."

"I quit Stars 'R' Us," said Jocko. "I'm joining Priscilla's new, unimproved Ordinary Little People. No offense, Felicity, but I don't wear pink *anything*."

Felicity looked startled.

"I'm quitting to join Priscilla's club, too," said Anthony.

"Me, too," said Lauren.

Ariel said, "I don't want to be a star if you have to act perfect all the time."

"I'm sick of parties," said Henry. "Washing cars is more fun."

"Getting dirty is fun," said Mary.

"Helping out is—well—not exactly fun," said Jason. "But people give you credit for doing it."

"I quit, too!" said Bethany. "Your club has too many rules, Felicity. Being a star is too much work."

"You'll be sorry!" said Felicity. "All you Ordinary Little People will be sorry."

No one listened.

Not even Priscilla.

Priscilla was too busy figuring.

Mr. Piper couldn't be her teacher for fifth grade. He couldn't advise a fifth-grade club. But if a club was open to all grades . . .

Priscilla raised her hand. She waved it. "Mr. Piper, there's one more thing!"

Her fourth-grade teacher *could* advise that club.